THE PIT OF FIRE

MAP OF AVANTIA

STONEWIN VOLCANO

KING HUGO'S PALACE

THE CITY

ERRINEL

THE JUNGLE VILLAGE

THE DARK WOOD

GRYMON
THE BITING HORROR

BY ADAM BLADE

ORCHARD

CONTENTS

I'd forgotten how much I hate this kingdom. The fields full of crops. The clear blue skies. The simple, smiling people, going about their petty lives.

Well, all that is about to change. When I get my hands on the Book of Derthsin, *I will have a whole new world of evil magic at my fingertips.*

King Hugo will pay for his smugness. Avantia will tremble. Its protector Beasts will suffer. But above all, it is Tom who will feel my wrath.

And as he perishes, it will be my smiling face he sees.

It's good to be back!

Malvel

THE BROKEN
TOMB

A bead of sweat dripped from
Elenna's brow. Her knuckles were
white on the hilt of her sword. Tom
circled, looking for an opening. She
crossed her feet, and he pounced,
bringing his own blade down. She
blocked, and tripped, landing hard
on her behind. Tom pointed the tip of

his wooden sword at her neck. "Got you again!"

Elenna growled, clearly annoyed at her mistake.

"What's wrong with you today?" asked Tom, helping her up. "You should never cross your feet in a duel – that's basic footwork."

"I know that," said Elenna, dusting herself off. "I suppose my mind is elsewhere."

Tom nodded grimly. It wasn't easy to forget the peril Avantia faced. Their Quest to the Isle of Ghosts had been a success in some ways – they had defeated several Beasts and returned safely. But in other ways, the danger was greater than ever. For they'd brought back with them an old enemy who Tom had thought was gone for ever – the evil sorcerer, Malvel.

"I can't help wondering where he is," muttered Elenna. "When he's going to strike."

Tom squared his shoulders. "And that's why we must keep practising," he said. "So we're ready."

The two companions were training in the courtyard of King Hugo's palace, as they had every day since they'd returned. And each day, Tom expected to hear news of some chaos breaking out in the kingdom. Malvel had returned from the dead, his evil spirit inhabiting the body of the wayward young wizard, Berric. The thought that their great enemy had risen from the grave to threaten Avantia once again was almost too much for Tom to bear.

A fanfare of trumpets sounded from the castle battlements. A voice rang out. "Open the gates for Captain Harkman!"

Tom turned, heart thumping, as the huge gates were drawn open.

Captain Harkman rode in on his great black charger, a plumed helmet on his head, his breastplate gleaming, his long red cloak spread over his horse's rump. The captain commanded the regular search parties sent out to scour the land for any trace of Malvel.

Tom and Elenna ran forward to greet him as he swung down from the saddle. The grizzle-haired old

warrior removed his helmet and
saluted them solemnly.

"Is there any news?"Tom asked,
searching the captain's face.

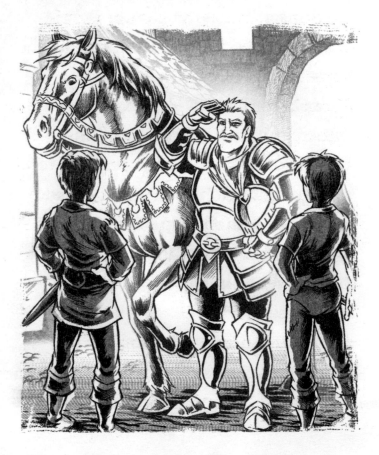

Harkman shook his head. "Not even a trace. My men have scoured the kingdom from border to border. We've questioned countless villagers. No one has seen any sign of Berric, or Malvel." He sighed, then added hopefully, "Perhaps he has fled Avantia for good."

Tom frowned. "It's possible, I suppose, but Malvel hates this kingdom more than anything. And he's a master sorcerer. If we haven't found him, it's probably because he doesn't want to be found."

Captain Harkman nodded. "I must carry my reports to Daltec."

"We'll come with you," said Elenna. They followed the gruff captain into the palace, guards coming to attention as they strode past.

The heavy doors to the throne room swung wide and they made their way down the long aisle to where the royal throne stood under the banners and flags of Avantia.

The throne was empty, of course. King Hugo had taken his pregnant wife, Queen Aroha, back to her home of Tangala. Any day, the kingdom expected to hear the heir had been born. Left in charge, the young wizard Daltec sat on a simple chair, reading over reports from across the land. He rose from a low seat as they entered, his youthful face worried.

"You bear ill tidings, Captain," said

Daltec, touching his own forehead. "I saw your coming as a darkness in my mind."

Captain Harkman bowed to the throne then stood facing Daltec, his hand resting on the hilt of his sword. "My search parties have not found Berric," he reported. "I believe it is time to recall the soldiers to the City. Guarding the Royal Palace should be our priority."

Daltec frowned and Tom could see that the wizard was uncertain.

"The captain is right," he said. "Malvel is certain to launch his first attack here." He pointed to the throne. "His ambition has always been to sit in King Hugo's place."

"And to crush all of Avantia under his boot," added the captain. "That must never happen!"

"You speak gravely," muttered the wizard. "But I—"

A deep rumbling *boom* sounded from beneath their feet and the floor of the throne room shuddered. Dust filtered down and the walls groaned. Tom rushed to the window and saw that one end of the stable block had collapsed. He knew that was the site of one of the entrances to a secret chamber beneath the palace.

"That came from the Gallery of Tombs!" he cried.

Tom led the frantic rush from the throne room and down a winding stone stairway to the dark tunnel that led to the Gallery.

He was the first to enter the great chamber, the captain at his heels and Elenna close behind. Daltec stumbled along in their wake, his heavy robes slowing him down.

Tom peered into the gloom, his heart thundering in his chest and his senses tingling. The carved walls of the circular chamber rose to a shadowy roof and Tom could just make out the nearer niches with their statues of heroes past. The bones of every Master of Beasts that had ever lived and died in Avantia were housed here.

Puffing, Daltec caught up with

them and made a pass in the air
with one hand, muttering a spell.
A host of crystals embedded in the
walls began to pour a soft light into
the circular chamber. Carvings of
women and men in armour emerged

from the darkness, armed with spears
and swords and battleaxes.

Two great tombs stood at the
centre of the Gallery. The larger tomb
housed the remains of Mortaxe the
Skeleton Warrior, but the lesser one

was the resting place of Tanner – first Master of the Beasts.

Tom let out a gasp of shock. The heavy lid of Tanner's stone tomb was cracked open.

"Who could have done this evil deed?" cried Captain Harkman, drawing his sword. "How could an enemy of Avantia enter this sacred place?"

Tom strode forward, sliding his own sword from its sheath. "It must have been something powerful to have done so much damage," he said, his voice echoing eerily.

"A Beast?" ventured Elenna, running ahead of Tom, her bow in her hand, an arrow on the string. "Oh!"

She stopped with a cry, staring at something beyond the tomb. "Oh, no!"

"What is it?" Tom rushed forward.

His heart missed a beat as he stared at the body that lay huddled on the ground on the far side of Tanner's tomb.

"Aduro!" he cried, instantly recognising the elderly wizard.

The old man lay motionless under his cloak.

Tom fell to his knees at Aduro's side, then eased the old man on to his back. Aduro's eyes were closed, and his face was covered in a fine layer of dust.

"Is he...?" said Daltec, his voice small and frightened.

Tom reached for Aduro's neck with his fingers, searching for a pulse.

Please, don't be dead...

2

MALVEL'S REVENGE

"Well?" Captain Harkman stood over him, his voice grim.

"I feel nothing," Tom cried.

Elenna crouched at his side, taking Aduro's hand. "He's cold," she murmured, her voice thick with grief.

Tom leaned over the wizard, his heart close to breaking. But then his fingertips detected the faintest flicker of a heartbeat.

"He's still alive!" he cried, looking up at Daltec.

"But who did this?" asked Harkman.

"I might be able to find out," Daltec said. He knelt down too, his hand resting on Aduro's wrinkled forehead. There was a long, tense silence.

"He is not physically injured," said Daltec. "I sense his slumber is of a magical kind."

"Malvel," muttered Tom under his breath.

Daltec lifted his hand from Aduro's brow. A soft blue light

shimmered between the young
wizard's palm and Aduro's forehead,
pulsing as it expanded into a
glowing ball of sapphire.

"What is that?" growled Captain Harkman.

"Aduro's memories," explained Daltec, getting to his feet, the ball on his open palm, blue clouds swirling within. "They may show us what happened."

Tom gazed into the coiling light.

The clouds cleared and suddenly it was as though Tom were looking through the old wizard's eyes.

He saw Aduro enter the Gallery of Tombs, staring this way and that as if looking for something. The former wizard paused at Tanner's tomb and touched the stone in respect. Then he turned abruptly, the Gallery seeming to whirl around him. A dark shape

burst from the walls – a ghostly
hooded figure that passed right
through the stone. Aduro moved
back as the figure glided towards
him. Then the shape became solid,
the hood slipping back, one white
hand reaching out with curled
fingers.

Tom gasped as he saw Berric's
thin, ashen face staring from
under the hood. He heard Captain
Harkman give a hiss of anger as
the fearsome figure moved closer,
its skeletal fingers grasping. But it
was the cruel gaze that caught Tom's
attention.

"Berric's face," he muttered. "But
Malvel's eyes!"

"Malvel's spirit has not completely subdued Berric yet," said Daltec. "But it is only a matter of time before Malvel reigns supreme in his body!"

"You mean he'll come back to life?" asked Tom.

"Yes." The wizard's voice trembled. "And then…"

Berric wielded a staff, pointing it at Aduro, then a bright purple light flashed. The vision wavered as the beam struck Aduro, and the walls of the Gallery spun, the ground rushing up. The last thing Tom saw was the robed form of Berric standing over Tanner's tomb, a fiendish light in his eyes as he brought the staff down like a giant hammer, cracking the lid.

The vision was fading fast, coming apart like blue mist, but the last thing Tom saw was Berric lifting something

from the tomb itself.

Then it was gone.

"What was that?" asked Elenna. "What did he take?"

Tom looked at Daltec, who was wringing his hands.

"What was housed in Tanner's tomb, Daltec?" growled Harkman.

Anguish was etched on Daltec's kindly face as he replied. "I never knew if the legend was true," he said, his voice trembling. "The *Book of Derthsin*."

The name meant something to Tom. "Wasn't Derthsin a sorcerer in the time of Tanner?"

Daltec nodded. "And a madman. He was a warlord, who meddled

with powerful evil magic. He supposedly collected his most terrible spells in a book written on Beast-hide pages."

"What sort of spells?" said Harkman.

Daltec's eyes widened in dread. "Derthsin was obsessed with a dark realm known as the Netherworld. No person has ever set foot there that we know. It is said to be a place where Beast fights Beast, of eternal misery and violence. Derthsin heard of magic that could open gateways to the Netherworld. He worked on charms to summon Beasts forth and bend them to his will – Beasts the like of which we've never seen."

Tom felt his blood run cold as the wizard spoke. "Do you mean Malvel now has that power?"

Daltec nodded dumbly.

"You wizards and lore-masters are fools, for all your mastery of magic," Captain Harkman muttered. "Why do you leave such deadly artefacts lying hidden around the kingdom? They should all be destroyed!"

Daltec gave him a grave look. "Our purpose is not to destroy, but to protect and preserve." He gripped his hands together, and Tom noticed that his knuckles were white. "Besides, there is no saying what magic is bound in the pages. To destroy the book may do more harm than good."

"What's done is done," said Elenna. "The important thing now is to stop Malvel before he has chance to use the magic in those pages."

Tom lifted his chin, his hand moving to his sword hilt. "While there's blood in my veins, Malvel will not succeed," he said.

3

A NEW QUEST BEGINS

After organising for soldiers to stretcher Aduro away, Tom strode out from the Gallery of Tombs, Elenna at his side, Captain Harkman and Daltec close behind.

"Malvel probably has no idea what he's dealing with," Daltec said, hurrying to keep up. "Derthsin was a far more powerful sorcerer. It may be that Malvel cannot even read the spells – they are written in Ancient Avantian."

"We cannot take the chance," said Tom. "I'll saddle Storm at once."

"And I'll organise troops," said Harkman. "We have to scour the kingdom and find Malvel before he even begins."

"No, stay here," said Tom.

"But—" Harkman began.

"If Malvel does manage to summon a Beast, and if we fall, this will be the first place he'll strike," said Tom. They came to the long hallway that led from the Throne Room. Tom paused, turning to look at Captain Harkman.

"Defend the City, Captain," he said. "Elenna and I will track down Malvel."

Harkman nodded. "But how will you know where to start your search? Malvel could have travelled anywhere."

Tom paused. Avantia stretched from the Icy Plains in the north, to the Ruby Desert in the south. From the Western Ocean to the borders of Rion in the east it was two days' ride. And Malvel could be anywhere.

Harkman's right. It's hopeless!

"Tom, your shield!" gasped Elenna. Tom shrugged the sturdy shield from his shoulder and gazed at the surface. The talon of Epos was

glowing slightly. Tom automatically
let one hand drop to the red jewel
in his belt – won from Torgor
the Minotaur. It allowed him to
communicate with the Beasts. He
sensed the thoughts of Epos the

Flame Bird at once.

Master, evil approaches like a dark cloud...

Tom looked to Elenna and Harkman. "I think I know where Malvel's heading," he said. "He's almost at the Stonewin volcano already."

Elenna paled. "It'll take us a long time to catch him."

Tom nodded grimly. Storm was fast, but they needed to cover so much ground. He touched the jewel again. "Epos, come to the City," he whispered.

"I wonder why Malvel is heading north-east," said Harkman, frowning. "All that lies in that direction are the borders of Rion."

"I don't know," said Tom, "but hopefully we'll catch him on Epos."

"Good luck with your Quest," said Daltec. "I shall visit the Circle of Wizards. Perhaps they will know how to break the sleeping spell that binds Aduro."

Daltec raised his arms, his robes swirling around him as he began to chant. The air shivered and there was a brief roar, like a distant wind. All around them Tom saw the shadowy and indistinct shape of a colonnade and recognised the mystical Chamber of Wizards. Then it, and Daltec, were gone.

Tom raced from the palace,

heading for the stables.

Shortly, the three companions were on the road that led to the palace gates. The city stretched out around them, peaceful and serene, the ordinary people going about their business.

With Elenna seated behind him on Storm, Tom stood up in the stirrups, scanning the eastern horizon. The black stallion stamped a hoof and snorted, impatient to begin the Quest.

Where is Epos? I hope nothing bad has befallen her...

And then, with the powerful eyesight of the golden helmet, Tom spotted a dot in the sky, like a distant fleck of fire.

"I see her!" he cried. Moments later, Epos soared above them, her golden wings spreading wide, flames flickering at the tips of her feathers as she circled and descended.

She landed on the road ahead of them, huge as a house, her eyes filled with flame, her great talons gouging the earth. Back on the City walls, Tom saw soldiers gaping.

Tom touched his fingers to the red jewel of Torgor. *Malvel has returned!* he told the flame bird.

Epos opened her beak and let out a cry of distress that echoed across the plains. Epos had good reason to hate Malvel – he had once forced her to

wear an enchanted band that filled her with an uncontrollable rage.

"Will you carry us into the far north?" asked Tom.

I will! Epos's voice rang in Tom's head.

The bird lowered herself to allow them to mount. Storm's hooves pressed deep into the feathers of Epos's broad back, until Tom instructed him to lie down.

With a powerful surge and a rush of wind, the great Beast took off.

Tom spread his feet and patted Storm's neck, seeing the horse's eyes rolling uneasily. "It'll be fine, boy," he whispered.

Epos turned north and the City

soon dwindled away behind them.
They flew over the Central Plains,
then on past the slopes of the great
Stonewin volcano, Epos's home. Wind
blasted Tom and Elenna, but the heat
of Epos's feathers kept them warm.

Tom kept his eyes peeled as they
headed further north. Could it be,
perhaps, that Malvel had fled the
kingdom completely? It seemed
unlikely. But it wasn't long before
they were skirting the mountains and
the border with the neighbouring
kingdom of Rion.

Below was a rough wasteland of
tall grass. A dark forest lay to one
side, and to the other, the pale waters
of a lake spread out, reflecting the

sky. Disquiet was growing in Tom's heart – the feeling that evil was not far away.

He saw a black shape in a flat stretch of grass, far below. Calling on the farsightedness of the golden helmet, he stared down. His blood chilled.

A cloaked and hooded figure stood there, arms outstretched, filled with menace. In one hand, it held a curious staff of white wood, carved with ugly symbols and with a horned moon at one end. The other hand held the book they'd seen in Aduro's vision.

"Malvel!" Tom hissed.

He could hear the wizard's voice

chanting evil words of power in an
ancient tongue.

"He's summoning the first of his
Beasts!" Tom called out. "Epos, we
need all your speed – attack now!"

Epos dived, her wings spread, the
wind howling as Tom and Elenna
clung to her feathers. The ground
raced up to meet them.

They were still high above when
Malvel turned suddenly and pointed
the tip of the staff in their direction.
A blast of lightning came searing up
towards them. Tom raised his shield
instinctively, and felt the blow strike
its surface with an ear-splitting
boom. He fell backwards, blinded
by a crescent of shimmering white

light that spread across the entire
sky. There was nothing he could do as
he rolled towards the edge of Epos's
body.

I'm going to fall!

He felt Elenna's hand snag his

sleeve, and pull him back to safety.

"Thanks!" he said, ears ringing. But straight away he realised something was wrong. Epos's feathers were suddenly cold, and coated in the same strange afterglow as Tom's shield. Looking at the surface he saw the six tokens – his connection to the Good Beasts – were deathly pale.

What does it mean?

"Epos!" Elenna cried.

Tom saw why she was so panicked. The flame bird's giant head was drooping, and the wind tossed her wings this way and that. Malvel's magic had blasted her unconscious!

Terribly slowly, they began to plummet.

FALLING FROM THE SKY

"Epos, wake up!" Tom yelled. When the Good Beast offered no response, Tom grasped the frozen feathers at the base of the flame bird's neck. He still had the might of the golden breastplate at his command.

He heaved back on the feathers with all his strength, feeling the magic swelling his muscles. Epos's head lifted a little and she pulled out of the steep dive.

Tom dug his heels in, swinging his body to the side, forcing the flame bird to veer to the right.

It's working!

The Good Beast's dive now took her over a curved inlet of the lake.

I have to time this perfectly.

"Storm!" Tom cried. "Jump!"

The stallion seemed instinctively to understand what Tom wanted from him. Storm turned and kicked off Epos's back, leaping down through the air. A great fountain of water gushed up as Storm struck the water. A moment later Tom saw his brave

steed resurface and swim for the
shore.

"Tom! Watch out!" He snapped his
head around at Elenna's warning cry.

The ground was rushing up. He took a deep breath, jumping sideways and rolling into a tight tuck. He hit the ground hard, tumbling over and over, his limbs gathered under him, his head spinning.

He heard the crash as Epos struck the ground. *Elenna?*

He stood, dazed, and saw his friend curled in long grass to one side.

Tom ran dizzily towards his companion, but Elenna heaved herself on to her hands and knees as he arrived at her side.

"Are you injured?" Tom cried.

"I think I'm fine," she said with a groan.

Storm surged up out of the lake and

trotted over to Tom, shaking his head and mane, water flooding off his flanks.

But they weren't all fine. Tom let his eyes follow the trail of broken grass to where Epos lay silent and still. No, not completely. Her massive feathered chest rose and fell softly. She was alive! Tom touched the ruby of Torgor, trying to speak to her, but he sensed only darkness.

"She is under my sleeping spell now," said a strange, reedy voice.

Tom spun around, drawing his sword.

The hooded figure glided slowly towards them, the hood thrown back. The red eyes in Berric's white face

glowed like fire-pits. The possessed
young wizard lifted his arm, pointing
the head of the staff towards them.

"Berric!" Tom called. "You have to
fight against Malvel! If you don't, he'll
consume you."

The red eyes gleamed and a smile

spread over the ashen face.

Elenna let out a gasp. "Tom, look!"

Tom watched in alarm as smoky green vapour rose from the hem of Berric's robes. The tendrils of smoke seemed to be oozing from the clothes, coiling around Berric's body, wreathing him in an ugly mist.

The smile faded from Berric's face and he stared down. For a moment, the fire died in his eyes and he stared at Tom in dread.

"Help me..." Berric's hand reached out towards him.

But the cocoon of green smoke tightened suddenly, like the coils of an evil snake. Berric let out a scream.

A blast of white light enveloped

the young wizard, sending Tom and Elenna reeling back.

The scream changed to cruel, wild laughter.

Tom blinked, trying to get the dazzle out of his eyes.

The robed figure had changed.

"No," Tom gasped as the face before him became clear. "No!"

Berric had vanished. In his place was Malvel, exactly as Tom remembered him.

"Yes, it is I!" Malvel's voice slithered like a serpent. He stretched his arms, his body growing, his eyes filled with a hideous glee.

"I have missed this!" he cried. "The feel of the wind on my face – the

earth beneath my feet!" His eyes shone with wickedness. "My enemy at my mercy!"

"What has happened to Berric?" Tom cried, lifting his shield, his sword ready.

"Berric?" Malvel cried. "There is no Berric! And soon there shall be no Master of the Beasts!" Malvel let out a low croak of laughter, brandishing the staff. "The power of my staff is formidable!" he spat. "It has put the six Good Beasts of Avantia into a deep slumber." He pointed the crescent-moon head of the staff at Tom's shield. "I used your hard-won tokens to aid my spell. Do you find that amusing, Tom?"

Gritting his teeth, Tom stepped forward. "Enough words, Malvel!" he cried, lifting his sword. "You should have stayed on the Isle of Ghosts – you have no place here among the living!" He took another step. "Let's end this once and for all," he shouted. "Fight me man to man!"

"Foolish boy," Marvel sneered, raising his hand, his fingers beckoning. "Come, then – come to your doom!"

With a ferocious cry, Tom leaped forward.

THE ENDLESS BATTLE RESUMES

Tom hurled himself at the robed wizard, shield up, sword flashing.

Malvel sprang sideways, swinging his staff so that the horn of the crescent moon caught Tom's sword and flicked it aside.

Tom stumbled as the razor-sharp horns of the staff whistled through the air and almost caught him a savage blow on the neck. He turned in mid-stride, aiming his blade at Malvel's chest.

Again, the staff came cracking down, driving the sword point into the ground and sending painful shock-waves up into Tom's shoulder.

He's more powerful than ever!

Tom dropped to one knee, pretending to be injured but with one eye fixed on his target. Then he wrenched the blade from the ground and brought it up in a slicing motion.

Malvel leaped back with an angry cry.

Powering up with both legs,

Tom sprang forward, following through with a series of stabs and thrusts that the wizard deflected by whirling his staff like a spinning wheel.

"Is that the best you can do?" spat the wizard. "You should give your sword to your horse – he has more brains than you!"

Tom ignored the jibe, forcing Malvel further back.

Malvel leaped away, shouting spells as he aimed the head of the staff at Tom. A blast of white lightning arced from the staff and Tom only just managed to raise his shield in time to send the forks of fizzing energy cracking up into the sky. The blow forced him to the ground, dazed, and when he looked up Malvel was gone.

"That way, Tom!" called Elenna, pointing. Malvel was racing for the trees that lined the grassland, his robes billowing.

Tom ran after him, but Malvel thrust out his staff. Spears of light sliced towards Tom, exploding on the ground and sending up a sheet of white flame that blocked his path and seared his face. Tom skidded to a halt and flung himself headlong in the grass.

I'm no longer protected from fire by Ferno's token! he remembered.

"Come and get me, coward!" called

Malvel from the trees.

Tom peered through the dying
flames. He had to change tactics.
If he approached across the open
ground, Malvel would pick him off.

"Elenna – cover me!" he shouted.

Elenna nodded, and strung an
arrow. The shaft flew towards
Malvel, who met it easily with a

blast of white fire. *But at least it's keeping him busy.* As Elenna fired again, Tom picked himself up and darted in a crouch, taking a wide circular route from the opposite side. Elenna loosed arrow after arrow, but with Malvel looking the other way, Tom edged nearer. He was twenty paces from his enemy when he stepped on a dry, brittle branch.

CRACK!

Malvel spun around and spotted him.

"Sneaky!" he cried, and blasted Tom with his staff. Tom ducked behind a tree and the spear of light crunched into the trunk with a flash, sending up a cloud of bitter smoke. As it cleared, Tom heard the tree creak ominously, and the branches above wobbled.

"I have you now!" Malvel crowed, pressing closer. "But you will grovel at my feet before you die!"

Tom saw his chance, pressing his back against the weakened trunk and straining with all the strength the golden breastplate gave him. The huge tree toppled and the Dark Wizard screamed, unable to move as the thrashing branches engulfed him. Tom ran along the trunk, leaping over branches. *Is Malvel dead?*

But in the silence he heard his

enemy's voice. He was whispering
something. Tom used his sword to
cut through the leaves, then found
the wizard lying on his back, with
the *Book of Derthsin* in his hands.

Tom brought the point of his
sword down against Malvel's chest.

"It's over," Tom panted. "Yield

now! The rest of this new life of yours will be spent in the palace dungeons."

Tom narrowed his eyes as the trapped wizard burst into laughter.

"Ever the noble fool," Malvel sneered. "Do you think I would engage you in a fair fight when I have so many allies at my command?"

Malvel slammed the book closed, and thrust an arm upwards. He let out a booming shout:

"Grymon! Arise!"

Tom staggered and fell from the trunk as a deafening peal of thunder cracked above his head. Again and again, the thunder roared, the noise like fists pounding Tom's skull.

The ground shook wildly, and a sound like clashing rocks made Tom fall to his knees. He heard Storm whinnying in panic.

"Tom! What's happening?" Elenna shouted.

Tom's fingers brushed the jewel of Torgor and instantly a horrible, grinding voice filled his head.

Quake before Grymon the devourer! Grymon of the black wastes of Netherworld!

Forgetting Malvel, Tom fought through the remains of the tree to see Elenna and Storm approaching. And beyond them, at the edge of

the forest, a huge bulky shadow
shouldered fully grown trees aside.
The moonlight caught it as it
emerged.

Tom reared back in disgust. A foul
reek filled the air, like the stench of

stagnant water and poisoned earth.

The Beast lumbered forwards, his body in the shape of a mountainous mole – his fur rank and slimed, knotted and tangled over a vast, bulbous form.

The Beast's huge head narrowed to a disgustingly fleshy snout with a pair of purple tendrils growing from it, each reaching tendril tipped with a raking claw.

The Beast lifted his grotesque head and Tom saw a single yellow eye staring at them.

The voice rumbled in Tom's mind, filled with malice and greed.

Grymon eats now! Grymon eats all life!

CHARGE OF THE BEAST

Grymon's cavernous mouth opened, his jaws bristling with long yellow fangs. Tom stared into the Beast's gaping red throat as Grymon bellowed. Fetid breath blasted in his face, sickening him, filling his mind with darkness and despair.

Grymon lumbered forward,

his massive claws tearing up the ground as he charged.

"Storm, get back!" shouted Tom, slapping his horse's rump.

Tom spread his feet, balancing himself for combat as the Beast careered onwards, single veined eye fixed on him.

"One good thrust into that eye and Grymon will be defeated!" he said to Elenna. She nodded, planted herself at his side and nocked an arrow.

"Stand firm!" murmured Tom, brandishing his sword with the point aimed for the Beast's eye.

"Always!" said Elenna.

As Grymon closed on them, the

long purple tendrils erupted from his fleshy snout, shooting forwards, the claws raking the air.

Elenna dived to one side, keeping hold of her bow as she rolled out of reach of the disgusting fleshy tentacles. Tom leaped aside, the snatching claws rattling as he parried them with his sword. His blade sliced into one of them, and he winced as thick slime burst over his face.

With a roar of pain, Grymon turned, his huge body churning the ground, clawed feet digging in, flinging clods of earth.

Tom spun his sword as a host of claws attacked him. He saw Elenna

leap to her feet and loose an arrow.
It glanced off Grymon's flank,
cutting a shallow groove in his flesh.
Enraged, Grymon twisted around,
his huge body turning with terrible

speed, his clawed feet like massive spades gouging the ground.

Elenna ran, Grymon's deadly tendrils snaking after her, the enormous claws snatching at her shoulders and back.

Tom sped after the Beast, the power of his golden leg armour giving him the speed he needed to grab at Grymon's stumpy tail. Clinging on grimly, Tom jumped, landing on the Beast's rump, fingers clutching at the slimy fur. If he kept his balance, he could race up Grymon's spine and pound his shield into the Beast's skull.

But Grymon must have felt him. The Beast's foreclaws slammed

into the ground, bringing him
to a shuddering halt as his hind
legs bucked. Tom lost his grip and
found his arms wheeling as he
somersaulted up through the air.
He crashed down into the trees,
grabbing at the branches to slow
his fall.

Smacked by heavy boughs and
slashed by breaking twigs, Tom
plunged down through the foliage,
landing heavily on his side.

Gasping for breath, he scrambled
up and raced into the open again.
Elenna was running hard, but the
Beast was close behind and she was
only one step away from being torn
apart by Grymon's snaking claws.

Tom cupped a hand around his mouth. "Storm! To Elenna!"

Storm was a little way off, rearing up and kicking with his hooves. He broke into a gallop, and Elenna saw him coming. She snatched at the dangling reins and swung herself up into the saddle.

Tom watched in relief as the brave horse carried her to safety. He speeded up to draw alongside Grymon's other flank as he thundered after her. He swung his sword at the huge body to get the Beast's attention. Grymon's head turned, the slimy snout throbbing, the tentacles whipping towards Tom. As Tom struck at the claws, ducking and weaving with all the skill at his command, he tripped on a tussock of grass. Before he could regain his balance, a tendril coiled around his neck, and tightened.

Dragged along at the Beast's side,

he struggled to get free. He couldn't draw a breath, and felt the blood pulsing behind his bulging eyes.

I'm close to blacking out....

His heart lifted as he saw Elenna, standing in the stirrups, her bow drawn, an arrow on the string. She fired, and the tentacle gripping Tom's throat exploded in a slimy mess. He fell to the ground and Grymon charged away.

Elenna continued the pursuit, close behind the Beast, stringing another arrow. But suddenly, the Beast's fleshy snout flared and twitched and the bloodshot eye rolled in suspicion. Grymon kicked out with a stubby rear leg and a clawed foot smashed into Storm's flank, sending horse and rider tumbling to the ground.

"Elenna! No!"Tom cried.

Grymon whipped around and lumbered towards the fallen horse and rider.

Tom, battered and bruised, stumbled across the uneven ground to help his friend. He summoned the power of the golden boots and jumped, right over Storm and Elenna, landing on the Beast's back. His feet slithered on the oily fur, but he steadied himself with his hands. Grymon bucked and shook, throwing him off, but Tom managed to twist in the air. He came down on two feet and drew his sword wearily. The Beast's huge eye glared at him.

At least he's forgotten about Elenna for a moment.

Grymon lifted his huge head and stretched his gaping jaws. Tom expected him to attack, but with a roar, the Beast sank his fangs into the ground, ripping the land open. He lifted his head and shook his snout, grass and earth flying in all directions.

What's he up to now?

Tom backed towards his friends. Elenna was gathering her bow from the ground, and Storm was shaking himself to his hooves once more.

"Are you all right?" Tom panted.

Elenna nodded. "Tom, how are we ever going to defeat this Beast?"

Grymon was still chewing at the ground, then using his forepaws to dig deeper still. First his head, then his bulging body, disappeared into the ground. Last of all, the tail vanished.

"Where's he gone?" Elenna whispered.

There was a rush and a rumble of earth. Tom saw a black crack open up in the ground, snaking towards them. He stumbled, flinging himself aside, but the chasm widened as it approached. *It's some sort of sinkhole...* He scrambled back as

the earth and rubble fell away into
unimaginable depths.

Elenna cried out in alarm, and

Tom's stomach dropped as he saw the ground give way under her. She slipped, her arms jerking upwards, her fingers clasping Storm's reins. The horse dug his hooves in, pulling back, neighing fiercely. But the ground was crumbling away quickly.

"Elenna, hold on!" Tom cried, rushing over the broken ground towards her. He was just a few paces away when her fingers slipped from the reins and she dropped soundlessly into the abyss.

Tom stumbled, his heart faltering. The ground had swallowed Elenna whole. And somewhere, down there with her, lurked Grymon.

UNDERGROUND PURSUIT

Storm backed off, neighing fiercely.

Tom ran to the lip of broken earth
and looked over, hoping that Elenna
had survived the fall.

He let out a gasp of relief. The
crater wasn't as deep as Tom had
feared, and it was half-filled with
the earth from the landslip. Elenna

was on her feet, shaking the dirt off her clothing, her bow in her hand.

"Are you hurt?" Tom called down.

"Only bruised," she called up. "Tom, you should come down here and see this! There are tunnels!"

"Storm, stay up here," Tom shouted to his horse. Before he made his way down, he scanned the trees. In the battle with Grymon, he'd forgotten all about the Dark Wizard. Was Malvel still trapped beneath the tree, or had he made a getaway?

There's no time to worry about that now...

Tom touched the jewel of Torgor, listening for the sound of Grymon's voice. There was nothing, but he knew they hadn't seen the last of the biting horror.

He descended the steep slope of the sinkhole, digging the bottom edge of his shield into the loose earth as an anchor to prevent himself from losing his footing. Elenna waited, covered in dirt, but thankfully unhurt.

As he reached her side, he could see what she had meant. All around him were the half-buried mouths of tunnels. It was as though the whole area was honeycombed with a network of burrows.

Elenna made her way to one of the gaping holes. Tom followed as she stepped into the gloom of the tunnel entrance.

"Did Grymon make them?" he asked.

"No," said Elenna. "Look."

Sure enough, drawing closer, Tom

saw the floor was smooth and firm and the curved walls were carved all over with the faint impression of drawings and writings.

"There must have been people down here," Tom said.

"Whoever they were, they're long gone," murmured Elenna. "Do you think we should return to the surface and track down Malvel?"

"Not before we take care of Grymon," said Tom. "Malvel is our true enemy, but we can't let the Beast remain on the loose." The ground trembled a little beneath his feet. "Did you feel that?"

Elenna's bloodless cheeks told him she had.

The walls of the chasm began to shake, scattering loose earth.

"He's coming," Elenna whispered, throwing panicked glances this way and that. "But where from?"

Tom felt for the ruby in his belt once more, and this time a voice crept into his head and made him shudder.

Food! Sweet, juicy food! I'm coming for you both...

From one of the tunnels, Tom heard the scrape of giant claws. Turning to face the entrance, he saw the shadows shift within, then a single yellow eye fixed on them. Thick drool spilled from a pair of gaping jaws.

We're trapped here in the open. Our only chance is to fight him in a confined space...

"Take my arm," Tom said, and pulled Elenna towards another tunnel entrance. "We have to keep together."

With a grunting roar, Grymon charged after them. Tom plunged into the tunnel, fleeing blindly. He ran his fingers along the wall, hearing their rapid footsteps echo.

After a while, he halted. "Shhh!" he hissed, his lips close to Elenna's ear. "Listen!"

Behind them in the darkness, he couldn't hear a thing. *Perhaps he didn't follow....*

Then his ears picked up the scrabble of huge rodent claws and the sound of heavy breathing. Grymon was in the tunnel, but he was moving slowly.

Tom felt for the wall, but there was only empty air at his fingertips. They must have come to a branch in the tunnel. Soundlessly, he drew Elenna aside and said under his breath, "He'll smell us as soon as he gets close enough. Be ready to run at my word."

Tom touched the red jewel, and Grymon's voice was in his mind once more.

Grymon likes the dark. Grymon hates the scorching light. Grymon

wishes he could bite the sun and make all dark. Tom shivered, horrified by Grymon's thoughts. *Netherworld dark, Netherworld good...but no food. No food for hungry Grymon. Here, plenty of*

*food. Grymon stay here. Eat the
whole world. Make many more
tunnels. Dig under cities. Bring all
down. Eat all life then sleep in dark
den under ruins.*

A wet snuffling filled Tom's ears.
It was close by.

Tugging at Elenna's arm, he ran,
a vile hissing and snorting at their
backs.

"Faster!"Tom gasped, urging
Elenna on.

He was sure he could feel the snap
of Grymon's tendrils close behind,
and the Beast's foul breath was all
around them like a disgusting cloud.

Emptiness opened out to Tom's
searching fingers.

"Side tunnel!" he panted, pulling Elenna into the opening.

They ran wildly through a labyrinth of intertwined tunnels. Tom lost track of time and distance. Using only hearing and touch, he had led them deep into the ancient warren.

"Wait!" Elenna gasped. "I think we lost him."

Tom strained his senses. There was a faint noise – but it didn't seem to be coming along the tunnel. He pressed his ear to the wall.

"Grymon must be in another tunnel close by," he said. "Maybe we can backtrack and find our way—" His words were cut short

by a sudden loud and ferocious
scrabbling. Tom felt the tunnel wall
bulge out. Grymon was clawing his
way through the solid earth to get at
them!

There was a crash as the wall burst

open. Elenna was pulled away as the collapsing wall forced them apart.

Tom fell back, holding his shield over his head as earth came crashing down on top of him, pinning him to the ground.

DUEL IN THE SUN

Tom lay stunned, crushed under the weight of fallen earth. Gathering his wits and using all the strength of the golden breastplate, he shoved upwards.

He squinted as bright sunlight struck his eyes. Grymon's attack had torn down the roof of the tunnel, leaving a gaping crack in the earth above.

Tom stumbled to his feet, coughing and gasping for breath.

Grymon was gone. Had the Beast lost their scent under all that earth? Had he returned to the surface, seeking out more prey?

Tom stared around, expecting to see Elenna, but there was no sign of her.

He clambered over the debris. "Elenna!"

He spotted her bow, sticking up out of the dirt. Her quiver was close by.

Tom dug frantically into the heaped earth. His friend was under all this weight of soil. He heaved a heavy clump aside and saw a pale shape. *A hand – reaching up out of the ground.*

He gouged out mounds of earth around the extending arm. Elenna's fingers closed around his wrist. She was alive!

He clawed away more clods of earth until Elenna's pale face appeared, streaked with dirt. She sucked in a breath, her other arm pushing up.

"I'm fine," she panted. "Go and deal with Grymon!"

Tom hesitated for a moment, but he saw the determination on Elenna's face. He nodded and got to his feet. The lips of the long crack were far above his head and there was no way to climb to the surface.

He heard Grymon bellowing and snorting – and mingled with the Beast's voice he also heard the desperate neighing of Storm.

His faithful stallion was in

terrible danger.

Tom crouched, tensing his muscles, his eyes fixed on the ragged lip of earth above.

Golden Armour, help me as you have never helped me before!

He leaped, releasing all the strength of his knotted muscles, springing high, spurred on by determination and anger. He burst through to the surface, landing and rolling across the broken ground.

Grymon had his back to him, the Beast's huge head swinging from side to side, the tentacles writhing through the air like long whips.

Storm darted back and forth, bucking, kicking up earth.

The Beast lashed out and snatched at Storm's leg, hauling the brave horse off balance.

Tom launched himself on to Grymon's back once more.

And this time, I'm not going anywhere!

He raced sure-footedly up Grymon's spine. The Beast twisted, releasing Storm, who scrambled away. Tom came to the base of Grymon's skull. The Beast's head jerked back, the quivering snout scenting blood and the sickening

tendrils arching back. Claws reached for Tom, who ducked and weaved from their deadly embrace.

"Not this time!" Tom shouted, whirling his sword. He sliced – *Snick! Snick!* – at the writhing claws, spreading his feet as Grymon tried to throw him off. He severed one claw, a gush of stinking fluid spurting out as Grymon howled and writhed in pain.

A second claw fell to Tom's spinning blade. The disgusting slime sprayed over Grymon's neck, and his bellows changed to shrieks of agony.

The Beast lumbered forwards, shaking his head, hurtling across

the ground in a wild panic. The
tentacles jerked and thrashed
wildly.

Tom saw the sinkhole looming
nearer. Was the Beast heading for
the tunnels? Did Grymon hope
to lose himself in the ancient
labyrinth?

Tom could hardly keep his
balance and he could do nothing to
stop Grymon's frantic charge.

He waited until the very last
moment before leaping clear.
Grymon hurtled over the edge of
the hole and plunged downwards.

He heard a horrible noise, like the
breaking of a tree in a hurricane.
Grymon's bellows stopped suddenly.

Panting, Tom ran to the rim of the sinkhole. The Beast lay at the bottom, his head at a strange angle.

Tom knew in an instant that Grymon's neck must have been

broken by the fall.

The Beast was dead.

A high-pitched whinny caught Tom's attention. Storm was at the crack from which he had leaped, head bowed to where Elenna was trying to scramble back up to ground level.

Tom ran over to them. Elenna was waving from below.

"A little help, please?" she called.

Tom took off Storm's bridle and let the reins down into the hole. Elenna grabbed them and he pulled her up.

"Grymon?" she asked.

"Dead," Tom said. "I'll show you."

He led Elenna to the sinkhole, the

horse following.

But the Beast's body had gone.

"Maybe he was just dazed?" murmured Elenna.

Tom's blood ran cold as the ground began to stir. He drew his sword once more, even though he doubted he had any fight left in him. The Beast's face broke through the earth.

"But..."Tom felt a frown crossing his brow."What...?"

For it wasn't the actual Beast at all, but a carving of its ugly head. It rose on top of a wide column, like a golden tree trunk, thrusting upwards and rearing high above them, taller than any of the trees

of the forest. The ground stopped rumbling and the giant pillar came to a halt.

"It must be a totem of some kind," Elenna said. Tom reached out to touch it, but before his fingers made contact, he felt a sickening wrenching in his stomach and flinched back.

"What's the matter?" asked Elenna.

Tom shook his head. It was fear! Pure, agonising fear. The chainmail of the Golden Armour usually protected him from such feelings of dread.

"This thing is evil," he said. He felt a chill pass through his heart.

"Tom, look!" said Elenna, grabbing his am.

Tom tore his eyes from the column to see the green grass around turning brown as if a wave of decay was spreading from the strange new landmark.

"Did Grymon cause this?" Tom wondered aloud. The tide of death was still spreading, the trees withering and dying even as Tom watched.

"Or is it one of Malvel's spells?" asked Elenna.

Tom stared around the horrible wasteland.

Malvel! Somewhere out there, Tom's greatest enemy was busy brewing spells for the downfall of Avantia.

"I don't know," Tom said to Elenna. "But this Quest will continue, and if it takes my life to do it, I'll stop Malvel from unleashing any more Netherworld Beasts on the realm." He lifted his sword and brandished it at the empty sky. "Do you hear me, Malvel?" he shouted. "While there's blood in my veins, I will hunt you down!"

THE END

CONGRATULATIONS, YOU HAVE COMPLETED THIS QUEST!

At the end of each chapter you were awarded a special gold coin.
The QUEST in this book was worth an amazing 8 coins.

Look at the Beast Quest totem picture inside the back cover of this book to see how far you've come in your journey to become

MASTER OF THE BEASTS.

The more books you read, the more coins you will collect!

Do you want your own
Beast Quest Totem?

1. Cut out and collect the coin below
2. Go to the Beast Quest website
3. Download and print out your totem
4. Add your coin to the totem
www.beastquest.co.uk/totem

Don't miss the next exciting Beast Quest book, SKRAR THE NIGHT SCAVENGER!

Read on for a sneak peek...

SHADOW PATH

"What in all Avantia is it?" asked Elenna. She gazed upwards, shielding her eyes.

Tom shook his head. "I don't know, but I don't like it."

Looming over them was a vast

golden column, as thick as a tree
trunk, with smooth, rounded sides
that gleamed softly. It was the
only sight to be seen in the lonely

countryside that stretched out around them; there wasn't even a signpost to mark the border between the Kingdoms of Avantia and Rion. A chill wind blew, and Tom felt a shiver run down his spine.

From the top of the column, a sculpted golden face glared down at them, frozen in a savage snarl. The face of Grymon the Biting Horror. Just a few moments ago, Tom and Elenna had defeated the Beast, and it had transformed into this strange golden edifice.

It feels wrong, somehow, thought Tom. *Almost as though it's...evil. And no wonder!* Grymon had been no ordinary Beast. Tom's oldest enemy, the sorcerer Malvel, had summoned the creature from the depths of the Netherworld using an ancient spell book – the *Book of Derthsin*.

And if we don't get the book back soon, there's no telling what other horrors Malvel will conjure to lay waste to Avantia.

"If only we had some sort of clue," Tom murmured. "Something to tell us where Malvel might now be headed..."

Elenna frowned. "Maybe we do," she said. Her gaze travelled down the length of the column, then she pointed at something on the ground. "What do you see there?"

Tom stared at the foot of the golden

structure, then gave up. "Nothing," he admitted. "Just rocks and grass. And the shadow of the column."

"Exactly!" said Elenna, grinning. "A shadow… But look, see where the sun is."

Tom glanced up, and saw that the sky was clouded over with a pale haze. Then it hit him. "A shadow with no sunshine! That's not normal, that's—"

"Magic!" Elenna interrupted. "I say we follow the path of the shadow."

Tom nodded. "It's the best lead we've got."

As they turned away from the column, heading back to where Tom's horse Storm was patiently waiting, a ghostly figure swam up out of the ground. It was a young man in blue robes, with the tall, pointed hat of a wizard. *Daltec!*

"What a relief to see you both safe and sound!" said Daltec.

"How is Aduro?" asked Elenna.

A cloud passed across Daltec's face. "See for yourselves." He stepped to one side and behind him appeared some sort of laboratory, the tables cluttered with books and vials of bubbling chemicals. The wizard Aduro lay on a bed in the midst of it all, his eyes closed, his face almost as white as his long hair and beard. Tom's heart sank at the sight of his old friend looking so weak.

"I'm still searching for a cure," said Daltec. "But Malvel's magic is strong. Whatever sleep he has put Aduro into is both deep and terrible..." He shook his head and smiled. "On the other hand, I have some assistance."

A girl stepped into view, perhaps five years older than Tom and Elenna. She had short black hair and was dressed in a red robe like Daltec's blue one. As she smiled at them, Tom caught a glimpse of something moving gently at her back – a pair of delicate wings like those of a butterfly.

"You must be from Henkrall!" said Tom.

"That's right!" said the girl. "The

Circle of Wizards has members from every kingdom. I am to be the new witch of Henkrall, the first since the fall of the tyrant, Kensa." She gave

Daltec a playful nudge. "Well? Aren't you going to introduce me?"

"Lyra, this is Tom and Elenna," said Daltec. "Tom and Elenna, meet Lyra. She's been so helpful. More helpful than I could have imagined, really..." He tailed off, gazing at Lyra with big, wide eyes.

Elenna laughed. "Daltec, are you blushing?"

The young wizard turned even redder. "I...er... Of course not! Wizards don't blush!"

Read
SKRAR THE NIGHT SCAVENGER
to find out what happens next!

Fight the Beasts,
Fear the Magic

Do you want to know more
about BEAST QUEST?
Then join our Quest Club!

Visit
www.beastquest.co.uk/club
and sign up today!

Are you a collector of the Beast Quest Cards?
Visit the website for further information.

AVAILABLE SPRING 2018

The epic adventure is brought to life on **Xbox One** and **PS4** for the first time ever!

www.maximumgames.com   www.beast-quest.com